The Hei

Also by Bernard Amador

To Know Å Fallen Angel:
Understanding the Mind of a Sexual Predator
Cyber-Eugenics: The Neural Code
The Rut

The Hei

ה

Hudson Mohawk Press
Latham, NY

Hudson Mohawk Press
595 New Loudon Road #138
Latham, New York 12110

www.hudsonmohawkpress.com
hudsonmohawkpress.blogspot.com
www.facebook.com/hudsonmohawkpress

ISBN: 978-0-9843040-6-6

Library of Congress Control Number: 2012951232

The Hei is an adaptation of the screenplay *The High*
© 2011 Bernard Amador (PAu 3-567-352)

Book design by Bernard Amador

Cover Image: *Bernard Amador*

Printed in the United States

For Bill

Life with you is effortless, like floating on the
Dead Sea.

Contents

Prologue

Sing Sing, 2025

A single bolt of lightning touched down in the Hudson River as I awaited my fate. The clouds crackled followed by a roar of thunder. There I was shackled in a bright yellow jumpsuit wearing teffilin and tallit. The walk I was about to take to the prison infirmary and my reason for going were giving me vertigo. I've walked this earth for forty years but this afternoon I felt like the thirty-three year old Christ walking the Via Dolorosa. It really doesn't matter that I'm a Jew, so was he. It does matter, however, to my chest-protruding over-confidant Israeli watch keeper Moses Sahid who has been by my side since I was extradited to the United States from Jerusalem and housed in Sing Sing.

Sing Sing sits in the town of Ossining, New York, approximately thirty miles north of New York City on the Hudson River. I am one of the two thousand inmates the maximum security prison houses. The name of the prison was taken from a Native American tribe from whom the land was "purchased". Its name is appropriate for my circumstances. Sing Sing literally means "stone upon stone". When this day is all said and done stones will be piled upon one another on my grave so that my soul will be bound up in the bonds of eternal life. It is my mantra that my beloved Palestinian mate Yaqub Abad be with me.

Muslim hip hop music flowed through the long corridor of cells as I took my final walk. Ali's arms rested on the bars as I passed. Like Christ I took a moment to rest and press my hand above the concrete wall. The sweat on my palm left an imprint beside the steel metal bars. When I arrived at Sing Sing, Ali made my acquaintance and tried to convert me to Islam. This was the last time I wished him well.

"Peace be with you, my brother!"

"Ethan, praise Allah in your journey," said Ali as he turned off his radio playing the hip hop music and grabbed a metal cup.

Ali took his metal cup and started to bang on the steel bars. Other inmates followed his lead and rhythmically banged. The bangs continued for six hundred and fifteen times marking me as the six hundred and fifteenth prisoner executed at Sing Sing. The last inmate executed at Sing Sing was Eddie Mays in 1963. The practice of execution at the prison was discontinued in 1972 after the United States Supreme Court ruled in Furman v. Georgia that the death penalty was unconstitutional. The death penalty returned to New York in 2008 through the back door when it was reinstated for those outcasts of society who took it upon themselves to kill a federal law enforcement officer.

Three court officers escorted me and Moses into the prison infirmary. A medical doctor dressed in a white coat and black rimmed glasses motioned to a nurse wearing a green surgical gown to prepare the room. The doctor checked the needles attached to tubes leading to intravenous bags. The nurse passed by me and headed for an adjacent room. I could see her through a glass window. She lifted a phone receiver off a desk and dialed as she held the receiver to her ear. The doctor sat on a padded stool. His face was hidden behind a surgical mask. The doctor got up and walked over to me. He did not say a word. Moses removed the shackles from my feet. The doctor went over to the wall and pressed a button. A screen rose to reveal spectators as they filed into the room next door, quickly taking a seat as they entered, eager to see the spectacle of which I was the star.

As I was mentally preparing myself to take my last breath, my thirty year old Palastinian beloved stood in his jail cell three floors above. My sixty-five year old Papa, Ira Hammond stood outside Yaqub's cell waiting for the door to open. The door clicked and opened. Yaqub exited the cell carrying tefillin and walked up to Papa. Both men stood outside the cell looking at each other in awkward silence. Papa looked at the tefillin in Yaqub's hands and spoke.

"You seem to have come to your senses."

"No thanks to these," said Yaqub as he lifted the tefillin.

"Those are not for play."

"You don't have to convince me."

"Do you know those were designed in the image of the first and second temple? An aerial view tells it all."

"Aerial view?" asked Yaqub.

iii

"Of the temple that housed the Holy of Holies."

"I haven't seen it."

"Quite telling," said Papa as he took a tefillin and lifted it up to Yaqub. "It's the image of a minim. A direct link to the song of the universe."

"Do you mean half note? Silence for two beats."

"Yes, only the sound of the universe," said Papa.

"At peace with the one," said Yaqub.

"Rests of the heart," said Papa. "It's like the fifth letter Hei symbolizing half. It's where thought and breath join. The point where time and space begin to form."

"Thank you for getting me out of here."

"I couldn't have done it without my son's help."

"Is he back?"

"They extradited him. Got back the day before yesterday," said Papa. "He risked his life for you and even though he found the people who were responsible they are blaming him. He's three floors below on his way to be executed as we speak."

"That's not what he went there for," said Yaqub as he handed Papa the other tefillin and ran down the hall away from Papa.

"They won't release you without my signature!"

"I have to stop it!"

"I've spoken to the Feds!"

"In that case you better hurry," shouted Yaqub as he disappeared down the hall.

Papa ran after him. It wasn't Yaqub's fault that I was in this predicament. I brought this all upon myself ten years ago.

Part I: Visionary Thinking

Chapter I

Central Park, New York City, 2015

On that bright Sabbath morning I took my usual stroll, along the perimeter of Central Park on Fifth Avenue. The heat of the sun permeated my yamulka. I could feel Hashem's presence. As I strolled along I drew near the Metropolitan Museum of Art. A blind man resembling a young Ray Charles sat on a bench feeding pigeons out of a small brown paper bag. The flock of birds fluttered around him trying to get what little the blind man had to offer. One of the birds was caught in a purple ribbon attached to a helium balloon that read: Happy Birthday!

The bird struggled, so I approached to release it from its constraint. The flock danced away and back toward the blind man who was taking pleasure in the cool breeze that the birds' wings wafted towards him.

The blind man stopped feeding the birds and listened as I scurried around to catch the entangled bird. Almost tripping over the flock I caught the pigeon and freed it from its bondage then moved on. Portal Jones, a forty year old homeless schizophrenic woman, stood on a milk crate peeling a golden delicious apple as I approached the entrance of the museum. Her paranoia penetrated my being as I passed. Portal's eyes darted around and followed me as I walked up to the museum entrance.

My passion and strong desire for what I've been trying to teach my beloved Yaqub was reflected in the art of my ancestral Jewish culture. There I stood as I did each week on the second floor of the museum mesmerized by Marc Chagall's 1923 painting *The Fallen Angel.* Meditating on the single eye of the falling angel in the painting put me in a trance as I mumbled my mantra for the day. After seeing Portal my lesson for the day was the need to humble myself. I repeated to myself, "The lowest outcasts are the tools of the divine." Right there right then on that special Sabbath, I could feel the energy as my body swayed. I could feel myself getting closer.

"The lowest outcasts are the tools of the divine...," that's until Yaqub nudged me.

"Ethan!"

"Uh."

"Here again?! Been looking all over for you."

Yaqub motioned to the Chagall.

"You've analyzed it for months."

"I tried explaining it to you."

"Others are trying to get a glimpse," said Yaqub as he motioned behind me.

Other museum patrons looked annoyed as I turned around and looked behind me. I walked away.

"Sorry."

"You have to stop this! Where are you going?!," shouted Yaqub as I took flight from the gallery.

I bolted for the stairs and Yaqub rushed after me as I ran out of the museum. Portal was now sitting on her milk crate. As I tried to run by she jumped up at me holding her carving knife in one hand and half peeled apple in the other. I backed away from the crazy woman as she shouted at me.

"Hey!"

I ignored her and moved on. As I slowed down and walked at a normal pace I turned and saw Yaqub descending the stairs looking for me.

"The angel calls!" shouted Portal.

I walked back up to her.

"What?" I asked.

Portal handed me the apple and exclaimed, "Eve's gift!"

She then lifted the knife and jabbed it into my chest.

My life flashed before me and I could hear screams and see the one-eyed angel circle around me. Pedestrians who witnessed the stabbing grabbed and restrained Portal. Yaqub caught me as we both fell to the ground. He cradled me close in his arms as blood poured from my chest and Portal screamed at the top of her lungs, "The burden is ours!"

Chapter II

Gracie Square Hospital

It's dark and cold. My eye lids blinked from the cold air pushing its way through the tunnel I am in. There was only darkness. My heart pounded and I could hear its pulsing in my ears. I rubbed my eyes trying to see. Pitch darkness. Am I dead? No, this had to be a dream. Wait, I could hear Yaqub's voice. It was faint. I stumbled in its direction. The walls were damp. I wiped the moisture on my thighs. Where the hell was I? Yaqub's voice got louder. He chuckled. The beat of my heart and love for him propelled me forward. I made my way forward but the tunnel was endless. My breaths were getting deeper as I gasped for air. I could only see darkness. I was dying or was I already dead?

"Open your eyes!" I shouted. Its echo vibrated in my ear canal.

Yaqub's voice faded as a screeching sound overpowered his voice. A continuous beep! My eardrums were punctured by the sound of a heart

monitor as I jumped up out of the ghastly dream
gasping for air. Two arms grabbed onto my shoulders. I
opened my eyes and the light blinded me back to the
darkness I fought to escape. I fought the blindness and
forced my eye lids open. The arms belonged to Yaqub.
As I struggled upwards he laid me back down. My
mouth was dry. I whispered through the dryness.

"I need...I need..."

"Shush. You need to rest," said Yaqub as he
pulled a sheet up to my neck.

Gracie Square Hospital sits in the middle of East
76th Street. I can't remember how I got here. I'm sure it
was by an ambulance. Nurse Rainer rushed in to
check the screeching monitor. She took a look at me
and exclaimed, "He's awake. I'll get the doctor."

Nurse Rainer exited the room as Yaqub stood over
me pinning me down by my shoulders.

"Happy Birthday," says Yaqub.

I tried to get up but I was weak and no challenge
for Yaqub's restraints.

"I need you to..."

"I know, there are thirty-two gates of wisdom...The
fallen angel...We've been over this already," said
Yaqub.

"This is not a joke," I get out of my mouth
between coughs.

Tears fell from my eyes as I turned away from
Yaqub. Dr. Blackburn, a tall and stern woman in her
late forties, entered the room and approached the bed.
Dr. Blackburn looked at the monitor and leaned into
my face.

"Showing emotion is good. You need to eat. Your
partner here tells me you are trying to attain peak
experiences," said the doctor.

I didn't respond. Yaqub pressed down on my shoulders.

"Marathon prayer, fasting, and sleeplessness is not the way. Do you think hallucinations will get you closer to God?" asked Yaqub.

"He's learning," I told Dr. Blackburn.

"Stop this nonsense already!"

The monitor screeched. Dr. Blackburn turned it off.

"You're upsetting him," said the doctor.

Angered by Dr. Blackburn's defense, Yaqub left the room. Dr. Blackburn turned to me.

"It's the third time we brought you back. We may not be so lucky the next time. We cannot let you use near-death to get your fix."

"He doesn't listen."

"You can show a blind man a picture but you can't make him see it. He has to use his other senses," she said.

"It's what's beyond the senses I'm concerned about."

"You can't force someone to learn. Eventually he'll get it."

"I'm running out of time."

"Get some rest," said Dr. Blackburn as she turned away from the bed and left the room.

Chapter III

Columbia University

A week later I stood in front of a classroom teaching my Comparative Religion course. As students entered the class Yaqub sat at a desk in the back of the room. I stood at a podium and lectured on William James' *Varieties of Religious Experience*. Naomi Strait was a frail and pale brunette who sat in the front row of each class ogling me. She was twenty-three, but looked pre-pubescent and in need of a roast beef sandwich.

"James argues in *The Varieties of Religious Experience* that one's personal religious experiences are rooted and centered in mystical states of consciousness."

Naomi quickly raised her hand. She was clearly the teacher's pet. No one else raised their hand so I called on her.

"Naomi."

"Does it have to be a religious experience?" she asked.

"Four requirements. First, words cannot describe it. Second, revelation is involved. Third, it lasts for about two hours, and Fourth, one loses control to God."

"Buddhism lacks a God," Naomi said as the bell rang.

The class got up and left. Naomi and Yaqub stayed behind. Naomi looked down at her paper titled: "Visionary Thinking". I know she couldn't wait to hand it to me. Yaqub stayed seated and watched Naomi as she approached the podium and handed me her paper. She was entranced and oblivious to Yaqub's presence.

"Professor, this is a survey of artists whose work reflect eschatological themes."

"James studied art briefly but never created it," I said as I took her paper. I laid the paper down and fidgeted with my notes. Naomi moved in closer.

"You're a professor of eschatology, but what about you?" she asked.

"Me?"

"With every ending there is a beginning."

"Reincarnation," I said as she leaned into me.

"Do you like to create, Professor?"

"Naomi!"

I stepped back and looked at Yaqub. Yaqub fumed as Naomi caressed my arm. Yaqub interrupted.

"Professor, have a moment?"

Naomi was startled. Embarrassed, she left the room. Yaqub got up and approached me mimicking Naomi, "...like to create."

"Oh come on. She's harmless," I said.

"You encourage her," said Yaqub as he approached me.

"Far from it."

"Since the semester began she's been after you."

"C'mon. I knew it was a mistake for you to take this class."

"She always has questions to get your attention."

"She's just a curious intelligent girl."

"Yeah, curious about you," I said as I tried to put my arm around him.

Yaqub pulled away.

"Don't," I said as Yaqub headed for the door. I grabbed Yaqub and pulled him close.

"Listen to me. You're the only one."

"Stop encouraging her. It only makes matters worse."

"I'll give her less attention."

"So you say."

"I promise. Now get going. You'll be late for your next class."

"See you tonight," said Yaqub as he looked at his watch, pecked me on the cheek and rushed off.

Chapter IV

Gate 15: Higher & Lower Awareness

I couldn't wait to get home. As soon as I got there I locked the door, dropped my briefcase and went straight for my prayer paraphernalia. I pulled off my jacket and covered my body in a tallit. I quickly wrapped my arms and forehead in tefillin. Opening my Torah to the Minchah prayer, Psalm 145, I slowly whispered it to myself in Hebrew and began to daven.

"I will exalt you, my God the King; I will praise your name for ever and ever."

Not too long after my body was covered in sweat and I was starting to feel drained, did I then feel a strong sensation that energy was surging towards me.

"My mouth will speak in praise of the LORD. Let every creature praise his holy name for ever and ever."

The weight on my body brought me to my knees as I began to flagellate then stop. As a puppeteer lifts the strings of its object of control, I could feel the energy lift my arms above my shoulders. I froze in an altered state of consciousness. This was the state I yearned for. If I gave it my all this practice would bring me to this state of true life I yearned for. I could feel the glow of a nimbus taking form around my head. The glow extended down through my body. It was my soul. This soul energy exited my body and would float above me. I was no longer in my body but was spirit. Achieving this portal is where I could enter the gates. The strength of my faith brought me to the gates. There I was sitting in a chariot racing through the clouds. Gates flash by. I rapidly approached a glorious gate. It was Gate 15: Higher & Lower Awareness. The gate opened. As the chariot entered my vision was interrupted by the phone in my apartment ringing. That jolted me back into non-spiritual reality. I opened my eyes and stumbled to the phone and answered.

"Can I help you?"

"It's David. Just heard from the Council for a Parliament of the World Religions."

It was David Rosen, my boss. David is the uptight Dean of Columbia University who was pushing fifty and miserable in all aspects of his life except his job. You name it--wife, kids, home, brought him nothing but pain and frustration. He loved his job for the title and that there really wasn't much for him to do. The only time he was involved was when one of the students in his department went off the deep end and had to be hospitalized for suicidal ideation. Lucky for him I kept my personal life outside the university or else I alone would keep him busy practically every semester. The fact that he was calling me at home told me that he had important news.

"And?" I asked.

"They approved your application and proposal. Your invitation to sit as a Council member at the next meeting is confirmed."

My heart was already pounding from being startled out of my vision.

"They've confirmed the Council location."

"Jerusalem," he said.

My head tilted up in praise.

"Oh. Thank you sir."

"Congratulations son!" he said.

As I hung up the phone, I shouted in Hebrew, "Let every creature praise his holy name for ever and ever."

I immediately went back to praying, resuming where I left off. I whispered my prayer forcefully and davened rapidly. My arms once again lifted above my head as I reached a visionary state. There I sat in the chariot before the glorious gate surrounded by clouds. The gate opened and the chariot entered. A hand grabbed my arm. I was five years old again and my Papa grabbed me out of his chair and threw me to the ground. I crashed onto the floor as my beloved dreidel spun.

"I'm sorry papa."

Yaqub entered the room and saw me hunched over on my knees and sobbing. Yaqub dropped his bag and ran over to me. He tried to lift me up but I was too heavy for him. Yaqub helped me to the sofa and fired into me.

"You couldn't wait."

"You're home early," I said.

"You just got out of the hospital."

"What time is it?" I asked.

"It's late. It smells sweaty in here."

Yaqub went over to the window and opened it.

"Skipping class is not a good habit to form," I said.

"You probably started as soon as you got home."

"Yaqub, I reached gate 15."

"I'll get your pills," said Yaqub as he exited the room and returned with a bottle. He took out a pill and handed it to me.

"Here, take this."

Yaqub went into the kitchen to fetch me a glass of water. He helped me take off the tefillin then went back towards the kitchen.

"Dinner will be ready in a few."

"I'm not hungry," I said.

"You like my curry. It's your favorite."

Yaqub disappeared into the kitchen.

Later that evening Yaqub and I sat at the kitchen table. Yaqub served me his splendid vegetable curry. As he sat across from me with a stern stare, I still felt myself coming out of the dream state. Yaqub lifted a spoon off the table and put it in my hand.

"Eat."

I didn't respond. This frustrated Yaqub.

"The pill is not good on an empty stomach."

I began to eat slowly.

"This is good," I said.

"I don't know if I can continue with this."

When I heard those words I put down the spoon.

"I haven't done anything."

"Really."

"Try me," I challenged.

"Ethan, you are addicted to mysticism and you are conflicted about being gay so you let that girl flirt with you."

"That's what this is all about," I said, "She's just a student."

"I was once just a student, too."

"C'mon. I'm not like that," I pleaded.

I slowly got up and went over to Yaqub. I hugged him. Yaqub was frozen. He stared off past me.

"Let go," he said.

"I will make it up to you."

"It better be good."

"I'll take you away," I said which quickly got his attention.

"Getting close."

"Jerusalem."

Yaqub was intrigued. His attitude turned.

"On your salary?" he asked in a playful tone.

"My application to the Parliament was accepted. I was just thanking Hashem when you got home."

"Then I should start packing."

"The dates are not finalized," I said, "I'll let you know."

"Just promise me you won't end up back in the hospital."

"I promise," I said as I hugged him and helped him put the dishes in the sink.

Chapter V

Columbia University

Naomi rushed to the podium as the bell rang and students left the classroom. Yaqub glared at me as he exited the room. I caught his eye and smiled back. Naomi was demanding and very persistent.

"Join me for a coffee."

"I have an appointment."

"Only a few questions," she said.

"Shoot."

"How did Jewish mystics go from a priestly class sacrificing animals to rabbis studying language?"

"That's in chapter five of the Carmody text."

"I didn't get that," she said looking puzzled.

"Take a closer read," I replied as I attempted to walk away.

She blocked me from leaving. I tried passing her on the right then left. She kept stepping in front of me.

I huffed and puffed but she continued to clearly be a bother.

"Ms. Strait, I have to go," I said and grabbed Naomi by the shoulders and pushed her aside and rushed out.

"What happened to Naomi?" she asked as she stood there. Then I heard her footsteps coming after me.

As I reached my car half a block away I could see Yaqub leaning up against it. He looked at his watch and began to pace. I stopped and watched a boy in his early teens wearing a keffiyeh approach Yaqub and hand him a flyer.

"For you," said the boy handing Yaqub the flyer. Yaqub refused.

"No charge?" asked Yaqub.

"Take it. Free," said the boy persistently.

"You're a bit young to be pushing stuff," said Yaqub as he took the flyer and read: "COME PRAISE ALLAH THE ALL MERCIFUL THROUGH THE TEACHINGS OF PROPHET MUHAMMAD, BLESSED BE HIS NAME."

"No thanks," said Yaqub as he handed the flyer back.

"The mosque is few blocks from here."

"Not interested."

"You know the teachings of the Prophet Muhammad? Blessed be his name."

"I am you," said Yaqub as the boy motioned for Yaqub to follow him.

"Come worship."

"Some other time."

"Care for your soul," said the boy persistently.

"You're a hard sell," said Yaqub as I approached the car. Naomi was half a block behind me. She ducked behind a tree. I didn't know she followed me to my car until later. Yaqub stood beside the passenger side door. He turned to me.

"Couldn't get away?"

"She's persistent."

"Don't get caught in her web."

"She almost lured me into the stabilimentum," I said as we both laughed.

The boy was still standing waiting for Yaqub. I motioned to him.

"Your friends are getting younger," I said as the boy just stared without a word.

"He's no one. Just some dealer," said Yaqub.

"You're going to be late for class."

"I wanted to see you off."

"Be home soon," I said as I caught Naomi peeking out at the both of us. I hugged and kissed Yaqub.

"Oh, merciful Allah," said the boy and ran off looking back as he passed Naomi ducked behind the tree.

Yaqub and I laughed as Naomi seethed with anger. We released our embrace. Yaqub also noticed Naomi as she looked at us.

"She's stalking you."

We both stood looking in Naomi's direction. She peeked out then ducked back behind the tree.

"Let me get going," I said and gave Yaqub another kiss goodbye, hopped in the car, and drove off.

~   ~   ~   ~

Later that evening Yaqub filled me in on what transpired after I left. He said Naomi stormed off and he ran after to confront her. He grabbed her shoulder and turned her around. While he was up in her face, he said, "You were following him. Why?"

Yaqub could see tears streaming down Naomi's cheeks. He took a few steps back and lifted his hand off her shoulder.

"Are you alright?"

"Leave me alone," she said.

"What's wrong with you?"

"Isn't it obvious?"

"Some things in life we can't have," said Yaqub.

"Why don't you go back where you came from?"

"I didn't hear that," said Yaqub sarcastically.

Naomi then shouted at the top of her lungs, "GO BACK WHERE YOU FUCKING CAME FROM!"

"I live here you STUPID BITCH!" said Yaqub as he looked away and took a deep breath in, "I'm trying to be your friend but you're not helping."

"I don't need your friendship. Besides, some things are achieved by force," said Naomi as she stormed off.

When Yaqub got home that afternoon we stayed up late in the living room cuddling on the sofa as he told me what happened. I couldn't believe him.

"Crying?"

"You should have seen her."

"Go on."

"She's in love."

"Love!" I said.

"Casanova better watch out."

"I'm not afraid."

"Before storming off she mentioned something about the use of force."

"Get out of here. You're serious," I said.

"Dead," said Yaqub as I bust out in laughter.

"She saw us kiss."

"That should put an end to it."

"One can only hope," I said as Yaqub got up and opened a bottle of wine.

We both sat up and drank into the evening.

~   ~   ~   ~

A half-filled bottle of wine stood beside another empty bottle. We both were tipsy. Yaqub laid back in my arms. I twirled my fingers through his hair as he looked up at me.

"The trip is coming up soon."

"Three weeks," I said.

"Have you lived in the homeland?"

"I lived there when I was younger. My parents traveled a lot," I said.

"Mine were killed by a car bomb inside the Holy City. I was brought here at five then returned. Now I'm back for good."

"When did you know?" I asked.

"I understood from the beginning. Just like my sexuality."

"When in Yeshiva, I drew a picture of Moses kissing God. The Rabbi tore it up."

"He couldn't see the love."

"He couldn't get past the idea. Besides we don't draw pictures of Hashem," I said.

"Like the conflict. No one wants to see it."

"No one wants to acknowledge or talk about it."

"Gay/Straight. Muslim/Jew. Israeli/Palestinian."

"It seems to matter," I said.

"Only differences matter."

"It's hard to name a similarity."

"Our diet is the same. We love the same God. If only people took the time to think, instead of relying on preprogrammed knowledge," said Yaqub.

"What's happening to the land? It comes down to who was there first," I said.

"They are arguing over rocks," said Yaqub.

"What's mine today may be yours tomorrow. There's a whole other world outside of this one and I can show you how to get there. We will be of one mind and body," I said.

"It already feels like we are there," said Yaqub as I snuggled him.

The next morning we were still on the sofa. Yaqub got up and puts his clothes on.

"It's too early to be up," I said as I yawned.

"I need to get some air."

"Come back to bed," I pleaded.

"Just going for a walk."

"Everything alright?"

"It won't be if you keep nagging."

"It's still dark out," I said as I looked at the digital clock that read four-thirty.

"I'll be back soon," said Yaqub as he grabbed his jacket and left the apartment. I turned over and pressed my face into the pillow.

Chapter VI

The Mosque

Aamil Murad, a fruit vendor, handed out produce from a cart in front of the mosque. Yaqub was hesitant to enter the mosque. He walked past the entrance, stopped, then turned around and entered. Aamil pulled out a small rug from his fruit cart and unrolled it. He knelt down on the rug. Two men grabbed fruit off the cart and ran into the mosque. The call to prayer echoed through the street. Allahu Akbar, Allahu Akbar...

Inside Yaqub and the congregation knelt down and prayed. After the morning prayers were over Yaqub was approached by the boy with the flyer who ran from him just the day before.

"You could come."

"Thanks for the invite."

"Did you like it?"

"Yeah."

"Come, meet father," said the boy and grabbed Yaqub's arm and led him out of the mosque.

The boy brought Yaqub to the fruit stand. Aamil looked at the boy.

"Father, Yaqub."

"A salaam alaikum."

"Good seeing you," said Aamil.

"Been a while. Trying to get back."

"Allah is always with you."

"Has friend. Wears yamulke," said the boy.

"If you come back you must follow the path of Allah, as Prophet Mohammed, peace be upon him, taught us," said Aamil as he reached into his cart and grabbed a Granny Smith apple and handed it to Yaqub. Yaqub turned his head and saw Naomi glower at him as she passed.

"I am here to pray. Not to engage in violence," said Yaqub.

"They kiss," said the boy as Yaqub glared at him.

"Your friend is welcome. We need help from within," said Aamil.

"I come to pray. That's all."

"Your parents would be saddened. Not from your relationship but from your lack of allegiance."

"Leave the dead where they belong, in peace."

"Their death was no accident," said Aamil as Yaqub took the apple. He bit into it and walked off.

Chapter VII

Israeli Consulate, New York

Lashem Yoel, the impatient rugged leader of Vessel, a Zionist terrorist group, sat in military fatigues in a van across the street from the Consulate while Achiezer Siskind, a twenty year-old faint-hearted follower of Vessel, tried spray painting a bathroom wall as part of his initiation into the group. He stuck a pin in the nozzle then shook the can. He then sprayed the scripture: "Return O Israel to the Lord, your God ~Hosea 14:2".

Lashem held his cell phone as he sat in the van. A few minutes later Achiezer climbed into the passenger's seat. Lashem turned to him agitated and spouted out in Hebrew, "I guess you couldn't be any longer."

As Achiezer opened his mouth to speak, Lashem pressed a button on the phone and the Consulate exploded. Screams were heard as debris flew everywhere and pedestrians ran for cover. The van screeched away from the curb. Police and fire truck sirens could be heard as flashing lights approached. As Lashem's van turned the corner the Israeli flag drooped off a bent flag pole and a cloud of smoke filled the sky.

Part II: A Portal

Chapter VIII

Gate 23: Negative Forces

I sat in a chariot surrounded by clouds. Gate 23 opened. It was lush and luxurious as a Salvator Dali painting. In fact, I was inside Dali's *Three Sphinx of Bikini.* I looked around and was amazed. I climbed out of the chariot and as my foot touched the lush green ground my clothes vanished. I grabbed a fig leaf off a nearby tree and entered the gate. Magnificent angels flew from under the wheels of the chariot and went before me.

"Hello."

"He he he he he...," the angels giggled.

"Who's he?" I asked.

"He he he..."

Passing a mushroom cloud I could see a second one off in the distance. Between the clouds was a large leafy tree. Its trunk was split. I followed the angels' giggles. Off in the distance I could see a figured leaning up against the bark of the tree. As I moved closer I could recognize the sillouette. The angels increased their speed.

"Wait!"

The Angels disappeared in the crown of the tree.

"He he he..."

As I grew closer to the tree I could see a fully naked Yaqub. He was unknowing. Yaqub leaned against the exposed bark. He was eating a Granny Smith apple. As I went to call his name I was jolted out of my vision by Yaqub shaking me intensely. Wrapped in prayer garb I screamed, "Stop!"

"I'm just preventing a hospital visit."

"Don't ever do that again," I snapped.

"Promise me I won't have to call an ambulance," said Yaqub as I pulled the Shel Rosh Tefillin off my head.

I tried to unwrap the Shel Yad Teffilin from my arm but I had tied it too tight. My arm was turning purple. I couldn't get it off.

"Help me."

Yaqub ignored me and left the room. He came back with a pair of scissors. He directed the scissors for the Shel Yad. I quickly turned away.

"Not with those!"

"You asked me to help you," said Yaqub as I ran from him.

Yaqub came after me.

"No."

"It's cutting off your circulation."

"My father gave these to me for my bar mitzvah, I said as Yaqub dropped the scissors and grabbed my arm.

Later Yaqub and I sat on the sofa watching TV. A new reporter was on the screen.

"Investigators are still trying to determine who is responsible for the bombing of the Israeli Consulate. They are asking anyone with information to please call the anonymous tip line displayed on the screen below."

"Things seem to be getting worse since 9/11," I said.

"The insanity was brought to this country," said Yaqub as he lowered the volume.

"You've had quite a few outings lately."

"Just getting some fresh air," said Yaqub.

"Recently you've been getting up and going out very early."

"I'm trying to get some exercise. Neuroscientists claim that walking expands the brain. How's the arm?"

"Fine," I said.

"Keep wrapping the same arm and you are bound to injure it."

"Shel Yad goes on the arm of weakness. The Shel Rosh the head."

"Oh," said Yaqub.

"It represents man's weakness. Muslims have similar practices."

"Your yamulke is my skullcap. You wear tefillin. I wear prayer beads. Some men wear beards," said Yaqub as I tried to hug him.

"Ouch."

"Still sore?" asked Yaqub as he put his arm around me.

"I saw you in my prayer," I said.

"Prayers are words to Allah. Not visions."

"The Kabbalah..."

"Enough already. Let it rest."

"Don't you care if we are together in the afterlife?"

"What! Of all creatures do ye come unto the males, and leave the wives your Lord created for you? Nay, but ye are forward folk, Qur'an 26:165. Or better yet, Leviticus, Thou shalt not lie with mankind, as with womankind: it is an abomination," said Yaqub.

"If you really believe that then you shouldn't be here," I said as we both sat for a moment in awkward silence. I watched Yaqub as he got up, grabbed his jacket and left the apartment. Frustrated that he left me alone, I too got up, grabbed my jacket and left.

Chapter IX

Childhood Home

When I arrived Papa opened the door. He lacked rabbinical garb and a yamulke. Papa was clearly no longer orthodox. He motioned for me to come in.

"Good Shabbos Papa."

"Happy Shabbos son," he said as I entered my childhood home.

That evening I helped Papa prepare the Sabbath meal. We first set the table.

"Mama always made sure this was done."

"Ever since Hashem took your mother away things have been different."

"I miss her too."

"We will be together again."

"I found someone special," I said.

"You could have invited him."

"Papa, I want him to learn the way first. Let us begin," I said as I picked up two candles and inserted them into holders then waved my arms in a circular motion saying the blessing, "Blessed are You, Lord our God, King of the universe, who has sanctified us with His commandments, and commanded us to kindle the light of the holy Shabbat."

I lit the candles and poured us a cup of wine as Papa continued the blessing.

"And there was evening and there was morning, a sixth day. The heavens and the earth were finished, the whole host of them. And on the seventh day God completed his work that he had done. And he rested on the seventh day from all his work that he had done..."

As we finished dinner Papa and I debated the state of the world.

"The world is different."

"Yes, but some people think it's the same. Our people have been struggling for years to have a secure homeland. They don't believe their own teachings," said Papa.

"You would think they would follow a true Jewish Science to achieve it. You know, without the bloodshed and use of force. Remember when I was a child of five and you threw me to the ground because I climbed into your chair?"

"I remember," said Papa.

"Force wasn't necessary."

"With time I have learned a great many things," said Papa as he could see the strain on my face. "It has harmed you. Please forgive me. I did not know then. Now I am wiser. I understand. We pushed you into your faith. I hope we have been forgiven."

"There is no need for forgiveness. I would not know spiritual enlightenment if it was not for your teachings," I said as Papa reached out and hugged me.

"Son, I'm sorry," said Papa as he rubbed my back, "I'm truly sorry."

Tears stream down my face.

"Don't, Papa. Because of you I know," I said choking back.

"Good then. Now come along. You're lucky I did not do as Abraham and place you like Isaac on the rock," said Papa as we both let out a laugh.

"Good Shabbos, Papa."

"No, Happy Shabbos," said Papa as he hugged and kissed me and we both got up and cleared the table.

Chapter X

The Mosque

A caravan of black SUVs and police vans pulled in front of the mosque. A team of FBI agents jumped out of the vehicles and stormed the building. One agent approached Aamil and his son. He forced Aamil's hands behind his back and wrapped a plastic tie around them.

"What have we done?" asked Aamil.

"What's wrong Papa?" asked the boy as another agent led him away.

They blocked off the entrance with yellow crime scene tape as the agents escorted members of the mosque out of the building into the vans. Women and children screamed at the agents.

Chapter XI

Gate 19: Separate Reality

Yaqub walked into the apartment the next day looking for me.

"Ethan."

I was not home. Taking off his jacket he approached the answering machine and saw the flashing red button. Yaqub pressed the button and listened.

"One message received ten forty-five am...Hey it's me. I stayed at my Dad's last night. Listen I just wanted to say I'm sorry. I won't pressure you or mention the Kaballah any more. I promise. Just do me one favor. This might sound weird but please stay away from green apples. See you later tonight. Love you."

Yaqub went into the kitchen and returned with a drink in his hand. He sat on the sofa, picked up the remote and pressed a button. The news was on.

"Police are still trying to determine who was responsible for blowing up the Israeli Consulate. So far there are no leads. Anyone with information is asked to call the anonymous tip line at the bottom of the screen," said the reporter.

The phone rang. Yaqub lowered the TV and got up to answer the phone.

"Professor Hammond?"

"No. Who's calling?" asked Yaqub.

"It's Naomi. Is Professor Hammond home?"

"He's not home at the moment."

"I know who this is," said Naomi.

"How did you get this number?" asked Yaqub.

"It's on the class syllabus, moron."

"No need for you to call."

"I have a question for the professor."

"It can wait until the next class," said Yaqub.

"I want to speak to the professor!" demanded Naomi.

"He doesn't love you. Never will. I suggest you don't call here again," said Yaqub as the phone receiver on the other end slammed down.

"Crazy bitch," said Yaqub as he hung up and returned to the sofa.

~   ~   ~   ~

Yaqub sat down and looked at his watch. It was twelve o'clock. He looked over at my prayer bag. He shut off the TV and went for the bag. Yaqub took out the tefillin gingerly and put them on. He draped the tallit over his head and kneeled down to pray. A few moments later Yaqub was deep in prayer and drifted away to another place. He felt a gentle breeze and found himself surrounded by clouds. A trumpet blew three times and the sound of a galloping horse drew near. As Yaqub stood a winged mule appeared before him and the sound of a heart, his heart beat. He was frightened. He couldn't believe his eyes. Yaqub could hear the sound of a voice he could not recognize.

"I will take you," said the voice as Yaqub's heart beat faster.

"No," said Yaqub as he felt his body drifting deeper away from himself.

Yaqub feared that he was dying.

"Do not fear. It is not your time," said the voice as Yaqub hesitantly approached the winged mule.

"Climb aboard," said the voice.

"But."

"No need to fear," the voice assured him as the winged mule charged at Yaqub.

"No!" yelled Yaqub.

"I will take you," said the voice as Yaqub fell through the clouds and descended from the sky as the beating of his heart pulsed rapidly.

As Yaqub kneeled down in prayer, he sweated profusely. Spooked, his eyes opened wide. He jumped up from the floor. The tallit dropped to the floor. He frantically yanked the tefillin off his body. One of the straps of the tefillin broke. He shoved the tefillin in the prayer bag. Yaqub couldn't believe what just happened. He rubbed his eyes then peeled off his clothing and headed for the bathroom. Just outside the apartment a team of FBI agents jumped out of a black SUV and stormed the building. Two FBI agents ran inside and up the stairs.

Yaqub ran the water in the shower and got in. The water cascaded over his body. He rubbed his face under the water as the agents banged on the door.

"FBI, open up!" shouted one agent.

Yaqub heard the banging and turned off the shower. As he reached for a towel, the front door burst open. The FBI agents stormed in armed with automatic weapons. Red laser illuminators danced around the walls. Yaqub ran into the living room tightening the towel around his waist.

"Get down!" shouted an agent, "Hands where I can see them!"

"What have I done?" asked Yaqub.

"I said down!"

"Wait a second!" said Yaqub as the agents rushed him. Yaqub's towel dropped as the agents tackled him to the floor.

Chapter XII

Childhood Home

Papa sat in his recliner as I sat across from him on the sofa. I got up to leave.

"I have to get going," I said as I looked at the top of the mantle where my dreidel and a pair of Tefillin sat.

"I can't believe you still have this," I said as Papa looked at the dreidel.

"Oh that. Your mother always kept it there for you," he said as I gave the dreidel a spin.

The dreidel spun on top of the mantle.

"She always told me what the letters meant."

As the top spun...

"That will only scratch the surface," said Papa as I grabbed the top before it stopped spinning. I laid it on the mantle and grabbed the tefillin.

"I know history," I said. "Can I have these for my friend?"

"Of course," said Papa as I carried the tefillin over to the sofa. I grabbed my knapsack off the floor and put them in it.

"OK, Papa."

"Sure you can't stay longer?"

"No, sorry. I have to get going," I said as Papa tried to get me to stay.

"Have the new archeological digs in the Holy Land helped you discover anything about the end of days?"

"No, Papa. I will see you soon. I really have to get going. I promised Yaqub I would be back by nighttime," I said as Papa got up from his recliner.

I hugged Papa and headed for the door. Papa followed and showed me out.

Chapter XIII

Federal Courthouse

After being interrogated by the FBI for twelve hours I followed a group of people into the courthouse and made my way to the pens. An officer escorted me to a thick plexiglas window. Yaqub sat staring at me. We both lifted phones and placed them to our ears.

"I got here as soon as I could. Your face was on every channel. The apartment was a mess. Just going for a walk to get some air?"

"I thought you wanted me to know God."

"Yes, but not to get into trouble. They are trying to indict you for conspiracy and terrorism. Besides, you could have stayed home."

"I wanted to pray at the mosque," said Yaqub as I held up the tefillin.

"You tried these? Mine were broken."

"Muslims don't wrap themselves in boxes."

"Tefillin."

"Whatever. I might as well wrap my head in aluminum. It serves the same purpose," said Yaqub.

"I brought them for you."

"No thanks. They creep me out," said Yaqub.

"So you have tried them. I'm going to leave them with the guard."

"Don't bother."

"Please take them," I said and motioned to a guard.

The guard walked over.

"Please make sure he gets these," I said.

"There are restrictions," said the guard.

"They're for religious observance," I said as the guard took the bag of Tefillin and walked away.

I turned back to Yaqub, "I hope your faith is strong."

"Now that I have those, I'm sure everything will be fine," said Yaqub.

"C'mon," I said as the guard came back and motioned to Yaqub.

"Time," said the guard.

"Can you extend it bit longer?" I asked.

"Time is time," said the guard as a second guard come up behind Yaqub and lifted him up out of the chair. He escorted Yaqub away from the glass partition and out of the room. Yaqub's case immediately went into a grand jury. I could not stay because grand jury proceedings are closed to the public and besides, I was called into Dean Rosen's office. Later, I was given what little formation had trickled out of the proceeding by the news reporter who covered the story.

Two court officers escorted Yaqub into a holding chamber in the courtroom. He was stationed behind a shield of glass separating him from the grand jury. The jury members sat in a booth opposite him. Yaqub looked around as the news van stood parked out front with its satellite dish reaching the sky with the news reporter beside the van giving blow by blow account of every detail that trickled out of the proceeding.

"We are live at the Federal Courthouse in Foley Square. If indicted the suspect is expected to have a swift trial. Little information is known about the suspect at this time. He has no previous record. He recently came to the United States and is believed to be a member of a radical student group. We will bring you more as the details unfold. Back to the studio...," said the reporter as Yaqub stood and awaited the reading of the grand jury's decision.

The jury foreman got up and walked to a podium. She cleared her throat and read...

"Case number 201551868. We the grand jury indict the accused on all counts of conspiracy, terrorism and premeditated murder in the destruction of the Israeli Consulate," said the foreman as the court officers lead Yaqub out of the court room.

Chapter XIV

Columbia University

David Rosen sat behind a huge oak desk. The room was framed with filled book shelves and religious artifacts. I entered his office without knocking and sat in a plush blue chair facing him. Before the seat could get warm David fired into me.

"We already have your replacement."

"But I didn't do anything wrong," I said.

"You are having relations with a student. Excuse me, ex-student who also happens to be a terrorist."

"Yaqub is no terrorist."

"Try convincing the authorities. This department has been disrupted with FBI Agents questioning all the faculty about you and your involvement with the students."

"There is nothing for them to report," I said.

"The university has already made its decision."

"What about my place on the Council?" I asked.

"Your replacement will represent the University."

"Hold on. Wait a second. That was my application and my proposal on Post-Millennial Eschatology," I said.

"Please clear your desk and don't forget to turn in your ID to HR," said David as I fumed. Pulling out my wallet I took my ID and tossed it on the desk.

"Sorry it had to end this way," said David having the last word, as I grabbed my knapsack and stormed out of his office.

I rushed down the hallway cutting my way through the students like a salmon swimming upstream. Naomi walked towards me. I tried to avoid her but she spotted me.

"Professor!"

I ignored her.

"Professor Hammond!" she continued as she approached me.

"Get lost. I'm no longer your professor," I said as I passed by her and continued to my office.

Naomi followed behind me. I reached my office and entered. She tried to enter as well.

"I have some questions...," said Naomi as I shut the door on her before she could enter. Naomi tried the door. I locked it just in time. She kicked the wall beside the door. Naomi sat on the floor outside my office waiting for me. After gathering my personal belongings I left the office carrying a box. Margaret Haas, a colleague of mine, spotted me as she passed in a hurry. Margaret was only in her forties and always in a peppy mood even though she looked much older in her string of pearls, outdated plaid skirts and cashmere cardigans.

"On to Philosophy of Religion! Catch up with you later," shouted Margaret as I fumbled with the box in my hands trying to close the door. Naomi jumped up to help me.

"Let me get that."

"I have it!" I said.

"I'll help you."

"I don't need your help. Please leave."

"I have a few questions about the readings," said Naomi.

"Here, take this," I said as I handed her the box. Naomi struggled with it. Oblivious to her chatter, I walked down the hallway as she trailed behind, "You didn't hear me."

"Hear what?" she asked.

"I'm no longer your professor."

"Come on, stop joking," as I took the box from Naomi and put it in my car.

I explained to her what happened.

"That's why I am no longer your professor," I said as I got into the driver's seat.

Naomi leaned into the window.

"It's all true then. You could really use a friend about now," said Naomi as I put the key in the ignition.

I paused for a second.

"Get in," I said.

Naomi smiled and hopped into the car and closed the door as I pulled away from the curb. She remained silent for most of the ride back to my apartment. I entered the apartment carrying the box. Naomi continued to trail behind me. I placed the box on the floor and peeled off my jacket. Naomi quickly made herself comfortable on the sofa.

"Would you like something to drink?"

"I'll have a beer," said Naomi.

"Is wine OK?"

"I'll take whatever you're giving," said Naomi as I went into the kitchen. Naomi looked around the apartment. The room was still in disarray from the FBI's visit. She got up and poked around. Naomi picked up my tallit and looked at it. I came back with two glasses and a bottle of wine and poured a glass for Naomi. She chugged it and handed the glass back. I poured another.

"Thought you'd be neater."

"I usually am. This is the work of federal law enforcement."

"What's with Grandma's shawl?" asked Naomi.

"It's a tallit. Part of my religious tradition. I'm usually praying by now."

"Am I interrupting?"

"No. Besides, Yaqub won't be home," I said as I took the tallit from her and draped it over the back of the sofa.

Naomi moved in closer to me. I put my arm around her.

"You have a plan?" she asked.

"I'll figure it out. Enough of me. Your story?"

"I'm from a small town up north. Farmland. Like everyone else, I had dreams of the big city. Large family. Nothing else to do up there but breed. But the pickings are slim. Not many hand me downs, either. All the cocks gathered in church on Sundays. Education was my ticket out of there."

"Your typical rural tale. Everyone is chasing a dream."

"I want more than a dream," said Naomi as she leaned into my arm.

After the third glass of wine we were drunk. Naomi giggled as I brushed her hair out of her face.

"I don't know what am I going to do without you there," said Naomi.

"Finish your education."

"And us?" she asked.

"We can be friends," I said as we remained silent. We stared into each other's eyes. I leaned in to kiss her. Our lips touched. I realized what was happening and pulled back.

"What's wrong?" asked Naomi.

"Everything. You gotta go," I said as I got up from the sofa.

"Why?"

"This isn't right."

"But I got rid of him so we could be together," said Naomi.

Her words quickly sobered me up.

"Got rid of him? What do you mean?!"

"Easy. I just called the tip line. Before you knew it his arrest was all over the news."

"Are you out of your freaking mind?"

"I did it for us," she said as she tried to pull me back onto the sofa and hug me.

"Get out!"

"Wait! Let me explain."

"There's nothing to explain," I said and grabbed her off the sofa and pulled her towards the door. She resisted. As I struggled with her she fought back and scratched my face. I threw her out of the apartment and slammed the door shut.

"Fuck you!" she screamed.

Naomi pounded on the door, finally leaving when I did not respond.

Chapter XV

Gate 22: Angels

Yaqub knelt down wrapped in tefillin. He leaned over a metal bed and pulled off a pillow case. He drapped the case over his head and began to pray. Yaqub's eyes were shut. He smiled as he achieved a visionary state. When he entered his vision he was dressed in white linen. He stood before a glorious gate as his body was illuminated by rays of sun. He looked through the gate at a new Jerusalem and Palestine. The land was in peace. Yaqub attempted to enter. His footprints trailed behind him in the sand. A trumpet blew. Before Yaqub could enter the winged mule appeared. Yaqub approached and mounted the mule. Milk flowed out of a terra-cotta jug attached to the mule's side. Yaqub drank from it. The mule took off and lead Yaqub into the new paradise.

Chapter XVI

Metropolitan Museum of Art

Portal sat on the bottom step looking for a handout as I climbed down the steps of the museum.

"Spare some change today?"

I stopped and reached into my front pockets. They were empty. I pulled out my wallet from my back pocket and only had plastic.

"Lunch is a better option. There's a diner close by," I said.

"Will it cost me?"

"My treat."

"I'm game."

"I'm Ethan," I said as Portal got up and followed me to the diner.

I held the door for Portal as we entered. We took a seat in a booth deep inside.

"Looks like a cat got at you," she said referring to Naomi's art work.

"You could say that."

"You're a man of God."

"That as well."

"I knew it when I saw you," said Portal as a waitress approached the table. The waitress looked at Portal and rubbed her nose. The stench was pungent. The waitress's eyes watered. Patrons looked around for the cause of the smell. The waitress sneezed.

"Bless you, dear," said Portal.

"What will it be?"

"Veggie Burger Deluxe. No cheese. No mayo," I said.

"God said, I have given you every green plant yielding seed for food, Genesis 1:29!" exclaimed Portal.

"For you, Ma'am?"

"I'll have the same," said Portal as I gave her a smile.

The waitress was eager to get away.

"Drinks?"

"Coffee."

"Make that two," said Portal as the waitress rushed from the table holding her nose.

As we ate I enjoyed Portal's rendition of biblical stories.

"You know Enoch and the fallen angels? It is the other story I want you to hear. The fall of the mightiest angel. Pride. Isaiah 14. O day star you are cut down. The mighty angel wanted what God had and was cast out of the heavens. His contempt led Adam to eat from the tree."

Her story prompted me to pull a paper out of my coat pocket. I unfolded the paper and pushed the plates aside and smoothed the paper out on the table. Portal leaned in to look. I showed her The Tree of Sefirot. She looked perplexed so I explained.

"Some say this is that tree. See there are 32 gates of wisdom made up of 22 letters and the 10 Sefirot. Adam knew of the knowledge of creation through letters. The Book of Creation tells of the 231 gates through which the world was created."

"Listen. God also created windows," said Portal as she pulled a yellow highlighter out of her nappy hair and turned the paper to landscape view.

She highlighted the fixed resistor symbol that ran through the tree. The symbol glowed.

"I'm no Einstein but it all looks like atoms and energy to me," said Portal.

"Yeah, we are all energy no matter how you look at it."

"It's no secret. Those who go with the current connect to the source."

"The path of least resistance," I agreed.

"People pass me everyday. I take note. They are afraid to look at me. They don't really see who I am. But I think you do," said Portal.

"We are not our shell."

"Or our scent. Do you have business at the Museum? You're there quite often."

"Nah. Just a favorite painting I like to meditate on," I said as Portal reached into her pocket and pulled out a Granny Smith apple. She handed the apple to me. The apple sparkled.

"You don't have to."

"We have been eating from the tree of the knowledge of good and evil for a very long time. It's about time we eat from the tree of life," she insisted.

"He warns against it. As a child I didn't always listen to my father," I said.

"A lesson for you to learn."

"I think so."

"His burden is not yours," said Portal as the waitress cleared the table. We both got up to leave and as we exited the diner the Blind Man made his way in and took a seat.

Chapter XVII

Federal Courthouse

Y aqub sat across from me at a table. I started to resemble the company I was keeping. My look was disheveled and unhappy. Yaqub was at peace with his incarceration.

"You don't look so good."

"I miss you, too," I said.

"You're going to miss me even more."

"How's that?"

"The prosecution is seeking the death penalty," said Yaqub.

"But you didn't have anything to do with it. I can't believe she did this," I said.

"Give me the facts. Identify the female element."

"Naomi called the tip line and reported you."

"She saw me in front of the mosque."

"You're pretty calm about this whole thing. You're the one who told me to watch out for the crazy bitch!" I said. "What's wrong with you?"

"Faith evaporates like steam," said Yaqub as I stood up.

"Hello! They can give you the death penalty. This has nothing to do with faith," I shouted as a guard approached.

"Back to the phones," said the guard as I followed him out of the room.

The plexiglas window was between us. I held the phone to my ear. Yaqub was on the other side of the window.

"What's going on?" I asked.

"I have been enlightened."

"Enlightened?!"

"Your boxes work," said Yaqub.

"Are you losing your freaking mind?!"

"I've achieved visionary thinking."

"They are seeking the death penalty and all you care about is enlightenment?!" I said.

"There is no need to fear death."

"What's wrong with you?" I asked.

"Ever since we met all you've talked about is the 32 gates of wisdom and our unity in the afterlife. Now I know what you are talking about. I thought this is what you wanted. Please be strong. There is something I need you to do," said Yaqub.

"I would do anything to make sure we are together," I said.

"I've seen you in my prayers. You are the sacrificial lamb, the key to peace in the Middle East and the world. You can resolve the conflict and ensure our union in the afterlife."

"You were having a mystical experience," I said.

"Contact with the divine involves more that just words. Sorry I argued with you. The feelings of release and enlightenment do not come from wrapping myself up in boxes. It's knowing that you will be there with me on the other side. To ensure we are together you must..."

"I've been there. You know I would do anything to be with you in the afterlife but what is it you need me to do?" I asked.

"There are 16 gates to the Temple Mount. If you multiply them by two representing an entry and exit, it gives you 32 gates. All 32 gates that lead to the Holy of Holies must be reopened. The last five spell the holy name. Remove the Dome of the Rock and open the gates! God's light must shine on the Temple Mount," said Yaqub.

"You're joking right?!"

"I've reached Gate 29, Gilgul, the reincarnation of souls."

"I've studied Kaballah all my life and I haven't gotten that far. You are probably not having true experiences. I'm sure you're hallucinating from the stress you've been under," I said.

"We are both physical and spiritual. Our actions affect only the parts of ourselves that are finite and bound in time. We are all part of Adam, a mirror image of the ultimate soul. Our soul gravitates toward the part of our bodies in action. Our genetic patterns and environment condition our soul type."

"They're teaching you Hebrew in here too?" I asked sarcastically.

"Since man fell from Eden we identify with the tree of good and evil. We have to rectify that to reach tikkun. We each must follow our own path. Your individual spark will not reincarnate because it has already reached tikkun," said Yaqub as I slammed down the phone.

I had heard enough. I got up and left.

Chapter XVIII

Faith

Yaqub was right. My faith was evaporating like the steam that rose from a manhole and dissipated as I walked along the streets of Manhattan. I admired the worshipers that entered Trinity Church as I passed. What happened to me? What happened to Yaqub? All along I pestered him to follow my faith. Now that he was where I thought I wanted him to be, I no longer know what I want. I took the subway back to my apartment hoping to reconnect. I entered the apartment, dropped my keys on the counter and picked up the phone.

"Papa...Yaqub and I need your help."

After my father agreed to help represent Yaqub I hung up and took a seat on the couch. I stared at my prayer bag and sat quietly in thought then began to whisper in Hebrew.

"Praise Adonai who is to be praised. Praised is Adonai who is to be praised for ever and ever."

I got up and grabbed my prayer bag. Taking my tefillin out I slowly wrapped the tefillin around my weak arm then stopped.

"Hear, O Israel: the Lord is our God, the Lord is One," I chanted unsure of myself. As I took in a deep breath and exhaled the tefillin slipped from my hands and fell to the floor. Without a prayer, I turned in for a good night's rest.

Chapter XIX

The Hei

The next morning I sat down in front of Yaqub and picked up the phone.

"Are you ready to talk sense?"

"I can't force you to believe," said Yaqub.

"I called my dad. He will represent you. If this is all true tell me something only I would know."

"You thought your childhood was difficult," said Yaqub.

"So does everyone," I said, still not convinced until Yaqub began telling me about my earliest memory as a child.

"When you were five you wanted what your father had, but you were scolded. Your Papa got up from a huge plush recliner and stood stern and tall. Papa closed the Torah and left the room. Your Mama was wrapped in an apron and saw you climb onto the recliner."

As Yaqub spoke I flashed back to my childhood. Yes, I was a five year-old. I played at my Papa's feet as I twirled my dreidel. Mama had prepared the room for the Sabbath. I could here her words as Yaqub spoke.

"You know not to sit in Papa's chair," said Mama.

Papa returned as I sat twirling the dreidel on his Torah. Papa grabbed the Torah in one hand, my arm in the other and threw me. I crashed onto the floor. The dreidel flew across the room and spun. I looked up at Papa as tears streamed down my cheeks.

"Sorry Papa," I said.

"When you get older this will all be yours, but for now," said Papa.

Mama grabbed my hand. She lifted me off the floor.

"Where's your dreidel?" she asked.

I looked around the room then pointed to it. Mama pulled me to the dreidel. The dreidel laid there with the Hei face up. Mama picked up the dreidel and explained.

"Hei symbolizes half. It joins thought and breath. Where time and space begin to form," said Mama as she handed me the dreidel. Your mother comforted you by teaching you about the Hei and the eternal return.

"You've been there," I said to Yaqub.

"I've witnessed the fall. The Koran teaches God generates beings, and sends them back over and over again, till they return to him. When the Holy Land is united we will return again together," said Yaqub as the phone dropped from my ear. I finally was convinced. I stared at Yaqub through the glass as tears streamed down my cheeks.

"No need for tears. You sit on the Council," said Yaqub.

"But the trip..."

"I know I can't go. But you can do this for us. Don't worry about me. We will be together as you wanted," said Yaqub.

I did not have the heart to tell him about losing my job and being removed from the Council. How could he see so much but not my current situation?

"What about your case?" I asked.

"I've seen our destiny."

"What else?" I asked.

"In my prayers?

"Yes."

"Jerusalem and Palestine are beautiful places. The world is at peace. All faiths worship together. There is no violence. The land is peacefully shared," said Yaqub.

"The new Temple must be breathtaking."

"Yes," Yaqub reassured.

"Like the original one Solomon built."

"There was no building," said Yaqub.

"Then how do you know it existed?" I dared to ask.

"The Temple is within. Wisdom and the Shekhina dwell among all men, women, children, gays, straights, Palestinians, and Jews," said Yaqub as I hung up the phone. Yaqub and I stared at each other for a moment then I kissed my hand and pressed it to the plexiglas and left. I passed Papa on the way out.

"The investigators can't find your student. She's disappeared," said Papa.

I didn't respond as I walked out. Papa took my seat at the window.

Part III: The Gates

Chapter XX

Jerusalem

My plane touched down on the tarmac at Ben Gurion Airport and I grabbed a taxi to the International Convention Center in Jerusalem. It was the second day of conferences for the Parliament of the World Religions. When I arrived there was a swarm of people making their way into the Convention Center. I entered the building with the crowd and approached the registration table. I scanned the table looking for a name tag for the Columbia University representative. I found it three rows back and reached in and snatched the tag off the table. As I was putting it into my pocket, an arrogant Margaret approached looking disheveled. She pulled a small luggage bag. Noticing her I slipped back into the crowd. She did not see me. There was a greeter standing behind the table. Margaret addressed her.

"Margaret Haas, Columbia University."

The greeter smiled as she looked over the name tags.

"We don't have a tag for you. Are you registered?"

"I'm presenting."

"Let me check the master list."

"I assure you I'm on it," she said as the greeter grabbed a huge computer printout. Margaret fiddled with her hair as I swept in behind her and grabbed her luggage. I strolled the luggage into the men's room and left it in a stall.

"You are on the list of presenters. Your talk begins in ten minutes. They are waiting for you in the Osiskhin Auditorium," said the greeter as I approached the table wearing the Columbia University name tag. Margaret frantically looked for her luggage when she looked down and realized it was gone.

"My bag. I just had my bag. Now it's gone."

"I'll call security. You can come back after your presentation," said the greeter.

"My notes and Powerpoint. I can't just wing it."

"You have a full house expecting a presentation on Post-Millennial Eschatology," said the greeter as I walked up to Margaret.

"Margaret, hi," I said, surprising her.

"Ethan. I'm glad you're here. David dropped this on me at the last minute. He asked me to fill in, with your termination and all."

"So you replaced me?" I asked.

"No, the new hire came down with some illness and couldn't make it," said Margaret.

"You seem a bit nervous."

"At this point, yes. I was going to go in the direction of conspiracy theories, but without my notes."

"You don't need notes," I said.

"I'm here less than five minutes and my luggage is stolen. Listen, I never got the chance to say how sorry I am or goodbye."

"No need to mention it. That's water under the bridge," I said as the greeter got Margaret's attention.

"Ms. Haas, they are about to announce you in the auditorium," said the greeter as Margaret glared. I grabbed Margaret by the shoulders and rubbed them up and down.

"Don't worry, I can help. We can present together."

"I'm glad you're here. This was your project to begin with."

"You have three minutes," warned the greeter.

"You just said ten," snapped Margaret.

"Ah...Let me handle this. Looks like that way to the auditorium," I intervened.

"Yeah, across the room to your right," said the greeter as she pointed off in the direction. I put my arm around Margaret and led her away.

Chapter XXI

International Convention Center

Margaret and I stood on stage in front of a huge audience. Lashem and Achiezer sat in the third row. I jumped into my presentation taking over the room as Margaret walked off to the side. The audience clapped as I began. A single stage light shined from behind me. The glow formed a nimbus that illuminated my head as I spoke.

"Nostradamus prophesized the apocalypse to begin 12/21/12. He was right about a lot of things, Napoleon and Hitler, but his prediction of a 2012 ending was wrong. There have been rumors of war which have come to pass and natural disasters which have plagued us as well as they always will. But as we can see, we are all still here today. I guess we will have to wait until 2060 to find out if Sir Issac Newton was right. What time has taught us is that Post-Millennial Eschatology must move in a new direction that supports a new beginning. Let's take for example what is happening right here in this Holy Land. The struggle between religious thought, Christian, Muslim and Jew. It is time for a new beginning to bring unity and peace to this land."

The crowed loved me. Their cheers roared. When they quieted down I continued.

"Current archeological evidence does not support the existence of a temple structure prior to Solomon's Holy of Holies. Before the Arc of the Covenant was brought to Jerusalem the ancestors of the Israelites would practice under the night sky. They moved into tents and then a concrete structure as technology advanced."

The audience was captivated. There was nothing but silence as they sat on the edge of their seats.

"Today there is a movement here to built a third temple by first having the Dome of the Rock removed, perhaps relocated to Mecca. But such a move would incite an apocalyptic war."

I was brilliant until…

"The Temple Mount is the original structure. The closest archeological evidence we have to an original temple structure is the 32 gates that lead to and depart from the Temple Mount. I suggest that a new temple be established by removing the covering structure and opening up the sealed gates so that people of all religions may come and worship under the day and night sky in the holy city."

There were simultaneous gasps in the crowd and the audience quickly turned as pandemonium ensued. There were clearly two factions in the audience, one for what I was proposing and the other against it. The factions began to shout in debate.

"This land belongs to our ancestors. There is nothing in the Torah about sharing the land," shouted an audience member as I tried to explain.

"There is no archeological evidence that proves the existence of a structure."

"There is no trace of our ancestors because the Waqf's clandestine digs are removing traces of the altar," shouted another who was followed by another, "After 1967 Muslims were given the right to administer the Temple Mount."

The factions began to argue amongst themselves.

"Not to destroy it," said another audience member as Margaret tried to interject to calm the audience, but it was too late. The audience refused to listen.

"Let us conclude with a civilized discussion," said Margaret.

"This land belongs to the Jewish people!" shouted another member.

"We can make the Old City a neutral cite for worship that can be shared by all," I said.

"Who invited this guy here?!" shouted another as the audience booed me.

An audience member began to sing Hatikva followed by his faction as another audience member sang Fidái. Both factions sang as they exited the auditorium. As the auditorium emptied out Lesham and Achiezer got up and exited with the crowd. Margaret and I walked off the stage and left the auditorium defeated.

Chapter XXII

Wailing Wall

The Old City was crowded with people going to and fro. The Dome of the Rock glistened in the distance. I stood facing the wall holding a small prayer book. My head was covered and I davened. Lashem and Achiezer approached me. They stood at each of my sides and prayed. Mumbling in Hebrew Lashem peered at me out of the corner of his eyes. He had never seen someone so devoted. I guess I made the Rabbis at the wall look like amateur believers. When I stopped praying, I leaned into the wall and kissed it before walking off. As I left Lashem and Achiezer followed. I could sense that I was being followed. I stopped and turned around.

"Stop following me."

Lashem spoke to me in English with a heavy accent.

"We can help you achieve your goal," said Lashem.

"Goal?"

"We want just as you do."

"Get to the point," I said.

"We heard you speak at the convention center."

"And?"

"You're right. We should remove the Dome. It's time for the gates to open," said Lashem.

"You haven't introduced yourselves."

"Lashem...Achiezer," said Lashem as both men grinned.

"If you can achieve that I'll listen. Lord knows the people here don't."

"We are part of a new organization that seeks change here and abroad. We have been working on this for quite some time and have a solution," said Lashem as he handed me a card. I took a look and flipped it over. The word Vessel was stamped on one side and a map of the Hishtalshelus, The Great Chain of Being was on the other.

"That is your key. Be there tomorrow night. Attendance confirms your membership. There is no turning back," said Lashem as he motioned to Achiezer. They walked off as I stared at the card. I took out my cell phone and called Papa. As I lifted the phone to my ear Papa answered.

"Ethan, where have you been? The trial is tomorrow. Yaqub won't say much, just nonsense. I'm trying to build a case for a mute. It's almost as if he wants the chair."

"I'm in the homeland."

"I don't understand."

"Jerusalem, Papa."

"What are you doing there? I need you here to talk some sense to your Yaqub."

"He knows what's right."

"My only option is a seven-ten-thirty evaluation," said Papa.

"He's not crazy."

"He sure is not acting competent. What are you doing there?"

"Yaqub sent me here."

"I'm sure you're there for a good reason."

"To remove the Dome and open the gates."

"Oy vey and you went? Does it hurt to be crazy?" asked Papa.

"Remember the story in the Talmud you always talked about. The four sages who went into the mystical orchard? Yaqub exited in peace like Rabbi Akiva."

"Ethan, those were only stories."

"Lessons both you and Mama taught me. Was Mama wrong?" I asked as my father went silent.

I hung up and shut off the phone.

Chapter XXIII

Federal Courthouse, New York

The television news van was parked out front with its satellite dish reaching to the sky. The reporter stood beside the van with the courthouse in the background as the camera rolled.

"The trial of the Consulate terrorist resumes this afternoon. Opening statements begin sometime today. More details about the suspect have emerged. He is foreign born and came to the United States shortly after his parents were killed by a car bomb in Jerusalem. It has been suggested, although sources have not confirmed, that he was a member of a radical student group. Live at the Federal Courthouse Building in Foley Square. Back to the studio."

Inside the courtoom Yaqub sat in the defendant's booth while Papa and the Assistant U.S. Attorney Dale Romney stood and addressed the court.

"The proceeding will now begin. Counsel," said the Judge.

"The prosecution is ready," said Romney.

"Your Honor, we are petitioning the court for a seven-ten-thirty evaluation of my client," said Papa.

"On what grounds do you make such a request?"

"May we approach?"

"If you must," said the Judge as commotion erupted in the courtroom.

Papa and Romney approached the bench.

"Your Honor, I am having difficulty communicating with my client," said Papa.

"What difficulty would that be?"

"I don't believe he fully understands the nature of the charges against him, and he is unable to participate in his own defense."

"Please explain," said the Judge.

"Your Honor, his language is full of word salad and symbolic references that do not make sense."

"You're not a psychologist," said Romney.

"That is why I'm petitioning the court to get one," said Papa.

"Most suicide bombers are religious fanatics," said Romney.

"He's not a suicide bomber. If he was he would have gone up with the Consulate."

"What makes you think he's any different from any other religiously motivated terrorist?!"

"You're out of line," said Papa.

"Come on now," said the Judge as he banged his gavel on the bench.

"My words were symbolic references, not religious. Besides if he was ordered to be executed today it wouldn't be possible without his competence ensured," said Papa.

"I won't argue against that," said Romney.

"Are you sure this is not just a tactic to buy time?" asked the Judge.

"No, Your Honor."

"This is a waste of the court's time," said Romney.

"I'm afraid I have to deny your petition."

"But Your honor."

"That's all counsel," said the judge as Papa and Romney took their places in the courtroom.

"The request for a seven-ten-thirty evaluation is denied. It is the court's opinion that such an evaluation is not necessary and will needlessly delay trial. This case will resume for trial in two days. This matter is adjourned until then," said the Judge as he slammed down the gavel a second time. The courtroom emptied as a court officer escorted Yaqub out of the holding chamber.

Chapter XXIV

Fakhriyya Mineret, Jerusalem

It was dusk when Lashem and Achiezer, dressed in army fatigues, rushed the building. The two aimed grappling hook guns over their heads and fired. The hooks reached the top railings. Lashem and Achiezer tugged at the cables and secured them. Both clipped themselves to the cables and put their guns in reverse to scale the wall. Lashem and Achiezer floated up the wall. A patrol guard approached in the distance with flashlight in hand. The guard surveyed the area as he flashed the light around. Lashem and Achiezer reached the top floor and hopped over the railing.

"This way," ordered Lashem.

Achiezer followed behind Lashem as they approached a large metal box that sat on a table. The box was attached to a huge metal bull horn. Lashem took out a small electric drill and unscrewed the lid as

Achiezer took a small detonator out of his pocket and handed it to Lashem. Achiezer wandered over to the door and checked it. He pulled over a long metal pole by the door to secure it, then returned to Lashem.

"It will detonate on the fifth verse. They will bear witness to the act of their Mohammed the prophet of Allah," said Lashem as he clipped some wires and attached the detonator.

The guard closed in as he shined the flashlight up at the arched windows. Achiezer ducked out of the light's path. The guard kept on the move. Lashem waited until the guard was off in the distance then drilled the lid back on the box. Lashem looked out the window to make sure the coast was clear.

"Now," ordered Lashem as he and Achiezer jumped over the railing and descended the building. They unhooked their clips from the cable and ran off as the sun descended in the distance.

Chapter XXV

Club Vessel

A light flickered and the name Vessel lighted up in orange neon as a crowed of club goers waited outside to get in. I approached the door in blazer and birkenstocks. A bouncer scanned me up and down and laughed. I handed the bouncer my entrance card and the smile disappeared from his face. He ushered me into the club as the crowd got rowdy. I followed the bouncer into the club as techno music blared. Lights flashed. The club was jumping with teens dancing wildly. A waitress passed by carrying drinks. The bouncer grabbed a cobalt blue colored drink off the tray and handed it to me. I lifted the glass in a toast.

"Purple door across the room," said the bouncer as he pointed toward the back of the club.

"Thanks," I said as I sipped my drink and made my way across the dance floor. The blue liquid spilled as the teens bumped into me as they gyrated. The bouncer vanished in the crowd as I reached the purple door. Another guard stopped me as I tried to enter.

"Just a second," I said as I pulled out my entrance card and showed it to him. The guard opened the purple door and let me in. As I entered he slammed the door closed behind me.

Behind the purple door there was Indian decor everywhere. Red, purple and gold plush pillows with satin broche were scattered around. The finest satin fabric for a Maharaja tied back with a golden tasseled chord. There clearly was a celebration going on. A drunken Lashem, Achiezer and others sat around smoking and drinking. In the center of the room was a model with a large replica of the proposed Third Temple in the middle. The group laughed then stopped when the door to the room opened and I walked in carrying an empty glass. I was immediately sandwiched between two guards. The room fell quiet. Everyone looked at me and whispered to one another. They obviously did not recognize me. I grew nervous. My drink had not kicked in. Lashem turned toward the door and saw me. He waved to invite me over.

"Professor! Professor, come!" shouted Lashem as Achiezer got up from beside Lashem. I approached and took his seat. Lashem wrapped his arm around me.

"Quite a place you have."

"Glad you decided to be part of our history and celebrate."

"What are we celebrating?" I asked.

"Vessel has been working on carrying out your desire for years. Tomorrow there will be a new Jerusalem."

"My desire of a new Jerusalem?" I asked.

"By this time tomorrow the Dome of the Rock will no longer be."

"You plan on accomplishing that by…"

"You said it yourself. The Dome symbolizes a covering of the Truth, the location of the Garden of Eden and the Rock of Abraham. Natural light must shine on the place to bring proper worship back to life," said Lashem.

"Tell me how you convinced the Palestinian leaders?" I asked.

"No convincing," said Lashem.

"Then how?"

"By a natural act of divine intervention."

"I don't understand," I said confused as Lashem got up and lead me to the model of the Third Temple in the middle of the room.

Lashem points to the Dead Sea on the model replica.

"We've planted a nuclear explosive at the Dead Sea fault that runs between Israel and Jordan to shift the plates beneath the earth. This will start an earthquake that will no doubt destroy the Dome of the Rock. A sign of the end times. The Third Temple will be built."

"You're joking, right?" I said.

"Give credit to your American Cinema Antagonist Lex Luther. If it wasn't for Superman Hollywood would be the modern Atlantis. In our case the Dome will be leveled for a Third Temple and a new beginning for the people of Israel. You're not Superman. Are you?"

"Yeah," I said, "My cape is being laundered."

"You must have been impressed with the work we did on the Israeli Consulate in New York."

"I'm impressed," I said mendaciously.

"We are true Israeli scientists, from archeologists to nuclear physicists, united to regain our place in history."

"That's a bit fanatical," I said as Lashem shrugged.

"They see us as a radical fringe group. But it's our history and our land. We were here first. The Dome will be full when the first shock hits," said Lashem as the group laughed.

I could see myself in Lashem, a flint of the spark I was now rejecting. The newfound information caused me to have a change of heart. I headed for the door. Achiezer immediately followed me. The guards also approached me simultaneously and pulled automatic revolvers from behind their backs. I raised my hands.

"Whoa! Wait a second."

"Professor, come have a seat," said Lashem as I stood firm. The guards shoved me back into the room. They searched my pockets and took my wallet, passport and cell phone. A guard handed the items to Achiezer then pushed me back toward the group. I stumbled back. Achiezer tried to catch me and dropped the items.

"Do I need to remind you that your attendance here tonight confirms your membership? You were warned there is no turning back," said Lashem as the Guard grabbed the golden tassel chord and tied my hands behind my back as Achiezer picked up the items.

~   ~   ~   ~

The next morning I was bound and facing a window as I davened. Achiezer sat on a chair nearby pointing an automatic at me. I stopped praying and faced him.

"You don't have to do this."

"I'm in too deep," said Achiezer.

"Untie me."

"I can't."

"I'm serious. I need to go."

"So am I."

"No. I mean I have to pee, toilet?! Washroom?!" I said.

"This way," said Achiezer as we walked toward the bathroom door. Achiezer reached down to unzips my pants. I immediately pulled back.

"I can hold my own."

"I'm not going to untie you," said Achiezer as I kicked the bathroom door. Achiezer lifted the automatic and pointed it at me. We stood looking at each other. I began to rock side to side then gave in.

"Go ahead," I said as Achiezer lowered the automatic and unzipped my pants. He reached in and took out my member. I wobbled into the bathroom, "I'll try not to soil the floor."

When I got back to facing the window in prayer Achiezer sat and looked at me in admiration. I stopped praying and took a seat across from him. I tried to distract him as I loosened the chord.

"I guess you don't pray."

"I'm not a fanatic."

"Probably when you want something," I said.

"I'm sure you have wants too," said Achiezer.

"Prayer is good for you. It allows you to reflect on why you are here."

"I don't need to be reminded."

"My selfish desire brought me here so that I could reach tikkun with Yaqub."

"Yaqub?"

"My partner. But your partner has helped me to realize that reaching tikkun without Yaqub and world peace is not my decision to make."

"Human unbending and spiritual enlightenment," said Achiezer.

"I guess you can say that."

"You express certain things easily," said Achiezer.

"Things shouldn't be difficult."

"If I'd expressed that to my father he would say I was crazy from watching too much American television."

"Homosexual relationships and Kabbalah are compatible," I said.

"My parents do not agree."

"My father was once a radical orthodox. His thinking changed over the years."

"Not all people can evolve," said Achiezer.

"They can with a true Jewish Science. The world and people change but yes some people continue to think the same. Take your struggle to achieve a homeland and the true teachings. Now that's incompatible," I said.

"Surely, there must be another way."

"True, Jewish Science teaches how to achieve things with peace. When my father used force with me as a child he did not know. It was with wisdom that he was able to teach me how to achieve spiritual enlightenment. He knows now," I said slowly as I took my hands from behind my back.

"I ran away because my father beat me because of my beliefs."

"And you believe?" I asked.

"Same as you. That two friends can be partners."

"You mean love one another," I said.

"I mean partners," said Achiezer as I revealed to Achiezer that my arms were free. Achiezer intensely held the gun on me.

"Lashem, he's the friend you speak of?" I asked.

"Yes."

"Abraham was a parent who thought he knew what was best for his son. On occasion he was wrong."

"He knew when to listen to Hashem," said Achiezer.

"It was his moment of enlightenment that changed history," I said.

"Letting go of tradition is not easy.

"All it takes is a new thought. Rabbi Alfred Geiger Moses was right, it's a Jewish Science that lets you see things from different perspectives and create an expansive new awareness for divine healing. Do you truly believe what you're doing is the solution?" I asked.

"No one ever asked me what I believe."

"You can't follow him blindly. You got to know him."

"We won't be responsible."

"Convince me."

"A detonator for the explosive is connected to the Fakhriyya Minaret. Once the call to prayer sounds it will all be over."

"Which Minaret?" I asked.

"At the Al'aqsa Mosque."

"This time I really have to go," I said as I got up off the sofa. Achiezer was confused. He stood up with me and held the automatic. He didn't have the courage to stop me as he let me go. Achiezer tucked the gun in his pants and handed me my wallet, passport, cellphone and car keys.

"Take my car. The blue Aveo.

"I don't know my way around."

"They'll kill me," said Achiezer.

"I thought you said he was your partner."

"I didn't say the feelings were mutual."

"I need your help," I said.

"In this land forgiveness doesn't go far," said Achiezer as I stared at him with a pleading look on my face.

"He can't hurt you unless you let him," I said.

"He'll be back soon," said Achiezer as we rushed out of the club and ran towards the Aveo and got in. Achiezer started the car and floored it.

"I'll get you to the airport," said Achiezer as the vehicle screeched.

When we got to Ma'ale Ha-shalom road the Aveo pulled into a checkpoint. Achiezer pulled his papers out of his shirt pocket.

"Give me your passport," said Achiezer as I handed it over. Achiezer rolled down the window as Moses, who would become my Israeli watch keeper, approached.

"We have to let them know to clear the city," I said.

"They will only detain us."

"Papers?" asked Moses as Achiezer handed the passports over. Moses looked in the vehicle.

I couldn't hold back.

"They are going to detonate a bomb and destroy the city!"

"Taking him to the hospital. Another American with Jerusalem Syndrome," interrupted Achiezer as Moses looked me over, "He traveled here without his medication."

Moses hesitated then handed Achiezer the papers back and waved us off. The car stalled for a moment then started. We drove away from the checkpoint and toward the Old City. Lashem approached in a van in the opposite direction. He looked over the divider. His eyes meet mine as we burned rubber. Achiezer sped away from the checkpoint. Moses and the soldiers ran to their vehicles. Lashem turned his van around and drove through the divider. He chased after us as the soldiers pursued. I pressed a button on my cellphone and put it to my ear. The phone rang on the other end and Papa answered.

"Hello."

"Papa. Yaqub is innocent. An international terrorist group called Vessel destroyed the Consulate. They are planning to destroy the Dome of the Rock."

"It will take a court order to...," said Papa as the call broke up in static.

"Papa! Papa!"

"You have already inherited the Earth. What more could you want?" asked Papa.

"To ensure Yaqub and I will be together," I said.

"Son, your soul will divide once again in the afterlife and require re-embodiment of those aspects of which you have little experience. You already know him, so your unity is assured when you pass on," said Papa as static interfered and the call was lost. I slammed the phone on the dashboard.

"Damn!"

"What?"

"We have to deactivate the detonator," I said.

"You won't get past a gate to the Temple Mount."

"It doesn't matter. If it detonates we will all be dead," I said as Achiezer turned the wheel. The car screeched as it swerved off in the direction of the Old City.

Part IV: Tikkun

Chapter XXVI

The Jewish Quarter

Achiezer drove onto the curb at the Zion Gate and we both jumped out of the vehicle. We entered the gate as Lashem pursued us. As Lashem entered Moses and the soldiers arrived. The Jewish Quarter was crowded with tourists. Achiezer and I ran through the crowd. Pedestrians watched as we ran by. Achiezer, out of breath, stopped and bent over. I stopped and turned around. Retreating, I grabbed onto Achiezer's shirt and pulled him forward.

"Take me to the Minaret!

"I can't go any further. There's not enough time."

"How do I get up there?" I asked.

"The main entrance is on the other side of the wall but you can get there through the Western Wall."

"The other side?!"

"Take this," said Achiezer as he handed his gun to me. I lifted my hands. Achiezer pointed to the Minaret.

"I'm a man of peace," I said refusing the gun.

"It's the only way. Diplomacy doesn't work up there."

"Friend."

"Be safe," said Achiezer as I hugged him and took off for the Minaret. Achiezer turned around and rammed smack into Lashem who inconspicuously lifted an automatic and pumped a bullet into him. Achiezer fell to the ground as Lashem disappeared into the crowd. A Muslim woman holding a baby approached Achiezer and screamed as she stood over him. A crowd encircled them as I ran off towards the Wailing Wall.

Chapter XXVII

The Wailing Wall

I ran towards the wall then stopped and frantically looked around. The plaza was full with a swarm of people covered in tallits. Some were in prayer while others celebrated. Two men came out of the cave carrying the Torah followed by a procession. I looked up to the Minaret and bolted for it. Lashem tailed me followed by the soldiers. Struggling through the plaza, I knocked over chairs and ran into some men as they davened.

"Sorry...Excuse me!...Sorry!...I need to get through!" I shouted as I became stuck in the swarm. Men were locked in arms as they danced side to side. A group of young men encircled me as I tried to pass under their arms. They began to sing in Hebrew.

"Hear, O my brothers in the lands of exile, The voice of one of our visionaries, (Who declares) That only with the very last Jew – Only there is the end of our hope!" sang the young men as I tried to break free. They wouldn't let me exit the circle. The chain unlocked and I could see an opening. I ran forward with great force as I stumbled and crashed into a row of chairs falling to the ground. The young men laughed as Lashem grabbed and lifted me off the ground. Lashem and I were face to face. Lashem reached for his automatic. I saw the gun as the young men began to form a new circle around us.

"Why in such a hurry?" asked Lashem as I pushed him with great force into the crowd of people.

Lashem tumbled back with gun in hand, accidentally squeezing off two rounds. The crowd yelled and screamed. Pandemonium ensued as everyone ran for cover. I pulled off my jacket and grabbed a tallit off a chair. Covered in the tallit I bolted for the Minaret, disappearing in the crowd. The soldiers closed in. The soldiers reached the wall and got the swarm under control. Moses saw Lashem running after me and pursued. I ducked in the cave on the far left corner of the plaza making my way thorough a crowd. A Rabbi handed out prayer books. He held one out to me. I pushed the prayer book out of the way and looked for an exit. Men covered in tallits davened. I reached the far wall of the cave and found no exit. As Lashem approached, I grabbed another tallit off a table and covered my head and proceeded in Lashem's direction, backtracking to the entrance of the cave. We passed one another as Moses following him reached the entrance.

"This way!" shouted Moses as others rushed in past him.

When I reached the entrance to the cave I bolted from the tunnel and ran through the crowd. There was commotion all around. Lashem heard the crowd's yell and turned around. He spotted me as I ran. The soldiers pulled tallits off the praying men as Lashem ran around the soldiers.

"Hey!" the crowd shouted as Lashem pushed his way through the crowd after me.

I ran into a third tunnel that led to the Muslim Quarter and passed an old man who struggled to make his way to the wall with the help of a cane. Lashem trailed behind me followed by the soldiers.

Chapter XXVIII

The Muslim Quarter

I made my way through the narrow passageways and pushed through the crowd of tourists. Vendors stood outside their stores and tried to get the tourists' attention. A small goat chained to a wall cried out. There was a small grandfather clock mounted to the wall that read eleven forty-five. As I passed a vendor he tried to sell me something.

"American, here come and take a look. For you, 50 shekels."

"No, I'm not interested."

"Forty shekels."

"Don't want. No," I said as the vendor grabbed my arm and held it tight.

Pulling my arm from the vendor's grip, I knocked into chairs and dropped the gun as I ran off. Lashem chased close behind as the soldiers closed in. I ran up a flight of stairs through an arched entrance to the

Temple Mount and before me stood the Dome of the Rock. The Dome glistened in the sun as a man sat and played a violin. Women and children were making their way to Al'Aqsa Mosque. I frantically looked around and saw the Minaret off in the distance. A young child approached me with an open string of post cards. He held his hand out begging.

"Help me. One shekel."

I reached into my pocket and pulled out a shekel and quickly placed it his hand. The boy tried to hand me the post cards but I pushed him away. I ran past a goup of men sitting in a circle. One man noticed me and got up and pointed at me as I darted for the Minaret. Lashem was close behind. When he ran past the group of men all got up and chased after him as the soldiers closed in. The women and children made their way into the Mosque and ignored the fuss. I stumbled and fell as I reached the Minaret. Lashem reached down and grabbed me as I tried to get up from the ground.

Chapter XXIX

The Temple Mount

Lashem lifted me up outside the Fakhriyya Minaret as I struggled to get out of his grip.

"You think you can stop destiny?" asked Lashem.

"You can't do this."

"Who's going to stop me?" asked Lashem as the group of men charged us. Lashem took out the revolver and pointed it at the men. The men ignored the revolver and continued to charge towards us. Lashem pushed me back down to the ground and pointed the revolver at me. As I cringed Lashem lifted the revolver and pointed it back at the charging group of men. The first verse of the call to prayer echoed in the wind as Lashem cocked the revolver to fire.

"Allahu Akbar, Allahu Akbar...."

The group of men all stopped at once, turned around to face the Kaaba in Mecca and dropped on their knees to pray. Lashem stood pointing the gun at the group of men. Time stopped as we heard the second verse of the call to prayer echo in the wind.

"Allahu Akbar, allahu Akbar..."

I looked up at Lashem. Lashem had a sinister grin on his face and chuckled.

"Thanks be to Allah," said Lashem as I jumped up and slammed into Lashem tackling him. We both tumbled to the ground. The gun fired. Lashem's head hit the ground and he fell unconscious. The revolver glided across the ground and landed in front of the praying men. I climbed to the top of the minaret and entered it as the third verse of the call to prayer echoed in the wind.

"Ash-Hadu an' La Ilaha Ill Allah..."

There was an old man on the floor praying on a small rug before the bull horn. I ran over to the old man and lifted him off the rug. The man pulled away.

"Turn if off!"

"Ah?! English no good," said the old man.

"You have to turn this off. It will detonate a nuclear bomb!"

"No...No," said the old man as he looked at me confused. The old man waved me off and dropped back down on his rug to pray. I looked around the metal box for an off switch but couldn't find one. The fourth verse of the call to prayer echoed in the wind.

"Ash-Hadu an' La ilaha Ill Allah..."

A dazed Lashem got up from the ground. He saw the soldiers approach in the distance. He climbed the Minaret as I frantically looked around then reached for the metal bull horn. I tried to destroy it unsuccessfully by pulling on metal mesh wire that lead to the horn.

The mesh wire was bolted in. I burned my hand on the wire as I pulled. I heard someone come in and turned around. Lashem was standing in the doorway. Lashem came at me and tripped over the old man. The old man jumped up and began shouting in Arabic.

"You don't belong here. Go!"

Lashem ignored the old man as he grabbed me by the shirt and slammed me against the wall. He punched my face as the old man watched. Lashem jabbed my stomach as I doubled over. The old man inched over to the metal pole that locked the door as I fell to the ground.

"Get up!" ordered Lashem as he grabbed me and tried to pull me off the floor.

The old man pulled the metal pole from behind the door, held it firmly and raised it above his head. The pole crashed down on Lashem's shoulder. Lashem dropped me as he grabbed for his arm and fell to one knee. The old man dropped the pole and ran for the door. Lashem got up and went after the old man. The old man was too quick. He got away as Lashem reached the door. Lashem turned around to re-enter when I jumped up and charged for the door shoving Lashem out the door and over the railing of the Minaret. Lashem's body tumbled down the side of the Minaret and hit the ground. The soldiers reached the Minaret and surrounded it. Moses looked at Lashem's lifeless body and kicked him to get up. Lashem was dead. I grabbed the pole off the ground and banged the metal box. The fifth verse of the call to prayer echoed in the wind.

"Ash-Hadu Ana Muhammadan Rasoolallah..."

I hit the bull horn with the metal pole. The sky roared as a mushroom cloud formed in the distance and the earth shook. As the earth shook the sealed walls of the entrance to the Golden Gate cracked. The sand between the stones fell and the stone wall crumbled to the ground.

"Ash-Hadu Ana Muhammadan Rasoolallah..."

There was pandemonium as the women and children ran all around the Temple Mount screaming and looked for safety.

Hayya 'Alas-Salah...," the call to prayer echoed as the men were still in prayer on the ground.

The soldiers stood firm surrounding the Minaret. The Minaret began to crumble. The group of men got up from the ground and ran.

"Hayya 'Alas-Salah...," echoed the call to prayer as Moses climbed the steps of the Minaret. The room shook. Cement crumbled from the ceiling and covered me. I dropped the pole and fell to my knees and prayed. Moses entered and saw me on the floor. He grabbed me and dragged me out. The room caved in as we exited.

"Hayya 'Alal Falah...," echoed the call to prayer as the stone walls sealing the arched entrance to the Huldah Gate crumbled to the ground.

"Hayya 'Alal Falah...," echoed as we left and the earth shook. The other soldiers and Moses escorted me away from the Minaret.

"Allahu Akbar, Allahu Akbar...," echoed as the Dome of the Rock trembled in the distance. Moses pulled me toward the Dome and the Fakhriyya Minaret crumbled to the ground behind us. The other soldiers followed us closer to the Dome. They all stopped and stared as the earth shook. The golden Dome wavered side to side. We watched and waited for the building to give in. The Earth gave one final strong rumble as the final verse of the Call to Prayer began then died out.

"La Illaha Ill...," was cut off as the rumbling of the earth stopped and settled quietly. The Dome of the Rock withstood the quake. The people cheered. I tried to walk off when Moses grabbed me by the arm.

"Not so fast."

"I was trying to stop this," I said.

"This was all your doing."

"I tried to tell you at the checkpoint that they planted a bomb to destroy the Dome."

"They?"

"Vessel."

"The night club?" asked Moses.

"It's really an underground terrorist organization."

"It sounds like you're relapsing."

"I don't have Jerusalem Syndrome!" I shouted and pulled away. Moses tugged on my arm and led me off toward an exit to the Muslim Quarter.

"Come along," said Moses.

When we arrived at Zion Gate Moses took me to a parked army truck. He opened the back door of the vehicle, motioning me to get in. I paused.

"I need to get back home."

"No time soon. Your friend Achiezer Siskind was found shot back there," said Moses.

"He helped me get away. I tried to stop this from happening."

"He's going to be alright."

"What about me? Please, I didn't do anything wrong," I said.

"Get in the truck," said Moses.

"You don't understand. I'm not responsible for this. I need to get back home. I need...," I said as I tried to make a run for it.

Moses ran up behind me and slammed his rifle down on the back of my neck. I fell unconscious to the ground.

Chapter XXX

Israeli Jail, 2025

The jail cell was dark. I sat on a small stool before a lit candle. A figure appeared outside the cell carrying a knapsack. It was Moses. The cell door opened and Moses entered. He stood over me.

"I'm tired of appeals," I said.

"So are we."

"Do I need to see a Judge?"

"You are being extradited to the United States," said Moses. "You're linked to those who destroyed the Consulate in New York, and you tried to destroy one of the holiest places in the world."

"That was not my doing."

"So you say."

"You are one of us. We're one and the same. I thought you were here to help me," I said.

"I will see that your execution is done humanely," said Moses.

"How is putting someone to death humane?"

"As long as it's done swiftly with as little pain as possible."

"Listen, my father is an attorney. He will help clear up all of this."

"You'll be in America soon. An American attorney has no status here. And your last request is?" asked Moses.

"I have two. Tefillin and Yaqub," I said as Moses reached into his knapsack and pulled out a set of tefillin and handed them to me.

"I can help you with these. Your other request, Yaqub, is impossible at this time," said Moses as I took the tefillin and began to wrap my weak arm. Moses left the cell and locked the gate behind him.

I davened before the candle in prayer and was transported to my childhood. I was five again sitting on the floor before Papa's chair playing with my dreidel. I watched the dreidel in a deep trance as it spun.

Chapter XXXI

Sing Sing

Papa followed Yaqub as he disappeared down the hall. The spectators were seated in the prison infirmary. The doctor connected me to three intravenous bags. My body lay motionless. The nurse turned to the doctor as Yaqub burst into the room. Papa was behind him. Yaqub ran to me. Moses tried to stop him. Yaqub threw Moses across the room. The nurse and the doctor stepped back. Yaqub reached me and yanked the intravenous tubes out of my arm. He tried unstrapping me. Moses got up and grabbed Yaqub, trying to pull him away. I opened my eyes.

"Yaqub."

Moses heard me say Yaqub's name and stopped. He stepped back. Yaqub tried to hold me up, unstrapping me. Moses approached the table and helped. Yaqub gently held me close. My eyes watered.

"I needed to make sure that we would be together," I said.

"We will always be together," said Yaqub as I began to fade out. Yaqub rocked me in his arms.

"Sorry."

"I'm not your burden," I whispered.

"I need you."

"Not your burden," I said as tears streamed down Yaqub's face.

I slowly closed my eyes.

Thought and breath were joined as I let out a final breath and embodied Hei. My eyelids slowly shut and darkness formed.

Chapter XXXII

Gate 22: Angels

It was dark and deserted. Yaqub held me in his arms. I was dressed in tefillin and tallit. Thunder roared as dark storm clouds rushed in. Lightning ripped through the sky. The wind blew violently. A flicker of light increased as it crashed to the Earth. Yaqub held me with one hand and wiped my face with the other as the light drew near. The burst of light radiated before us. All was silent. Yaqub couldn't believe his eyes. Floating upside down before him was a one-eyed angel. She was flaming red with a glowing yellow eye. A nimbus around the angel flickered. She looked at Yaqub for a moment and hesitated. Yaqub looked back at her as tears streamed down his face. The angel floated above me and settled down on my body. Her body melded into mine. Her single eye rested in the center of my forehead. Yaqub pulled me closer as droplets of rain fell from the sky. The droplets of rain increased to a downpour. Flashing lightning shot through the sky and a final roar of thunder echoed in my ear. The lightning flickered like the reels of film though a projector as I saw hospital staff run and pushed a body on a gurney down a corridor. My eyelids opened and shut as lights above flashed by. I could hear Dr. Blackburn.

"Station one! Oxygen."

The hospital staff rolled the gurney into station two. A monitor was quickly attached to the body.

There was the sound of the machine flat lining.

"We're loosing him. Defibrillator! Clear! Clear!" shouted Dr. Blackburn as the defibrillator sent a shock.

The body jolted.

"Again...clear!"

The defibrillator sent a second shock.

The machine beeped.

The sound of life.

"Pulse!"

Chapter XXXIII

Gracie Square Hospital

The body was Yaqub's. He laid on a hospital bed hooked up to a heart monitor. He was soaked in sweat. The machine screeched. Yaqub jumped up out of a dream and gasped for air. Papa, Naomi and I were by his side. I placed my hands on Yaqub's shoulders. A nurse rushed in and checked the screeching monitor.

"By gosh another awakening. I'll get the doctor," said the nurse.

The nurse left and I held Yaqub's shoulders. Yaqub tried to get up. I restrained him.

"The fifth letter!" said Yaqub.

"I know. Try to rest," I said as Yaqub choked back tears.

"Thought I lost you," said Yaqub.

"You came in just in time. They had only administered the sodium thiopental. A few minutes later and I would have been gone," I said as I reached into my pocket. "I brought you something."

I handed Yaqub a postcard.

Yaqub looked at it. It was a blank postcard.

"The other side," I said as Yaqub flipped it over and saw Marc Chagall's painting *The Falling Angel.*

His eyes teared up.

"Saw it all. You were there."

"Russia. Chagall's homeland?" I asked.

"No, Jerusalem."

"Yes, I was there."

"You found out who was responsible," said Yaqub.

"Yes, that also."

"I was arrested for the bombing," said Yaqub as he got excited.

"Settle down," I said as Yaqub noticed Naomi in the room.

"What's she doing here? She reported me."

"That's no way to treat a friend," I said.

"Friend?!"

"Calm down. She came forward and told the truth," I said as Dr. Blackburn entered the room.

"I see you're picking up his habits," Dr. Blackburn said to Yaqub.

"He's just using his other senses," I said as Yaqub didn't respond.

"One of you may not be so lucky. Please do not let there be a next time. Get some rest," said Dr. Blackburn as she left the room.

Epilogue

Metropolitan Museum of Art

It was a bright sunny day. Portal sat on her crate and waved to me as I walked down the stairs from the Metropolitan Museum of Art. Portal was cleaned up and less disheveled looking. She was happy to see me.

"Man of God!"

"Looking good," I said.

"So do you."

"Feeling alive."

"Most people aren't," said Portal.

"I'm finishing up a project and looking for people with strong spiritual views to come and speak to my class on the Messianic age."

"We're in it."

"So I can count on you?" I asked.

"Wouldn't miss it."

"I'll touch base with you when Yaqub and I get back from Jerusalem."

"Sounds like you got what you wanted."

"And more," I said.

"Never forget pride and the mightiest angel," Portal warned as I nodded my head and continued toward Central Park.

As I walked along the park a family celebrated their son's fifth birthday. Children ran around chasing one another. A dog ran after. Helium balloons were everywhere. The family sang.

"Happy Birthday to you!...Happy Birthday to you!...Happy birthday dear Ethan...Happy Birthday to you!"

They all cheered. As I peered in closer I saw a boy who resembled me when I was five. He was holding a balloon and about to blow out a candle shaped in the number five. The boy took in a deep breath and as he blew out the candle the balloon escaped his grasp. I smiled and turned away. I continued to walk along the park. The blind man sat on his bench. As I passed, the blind man looked up to the balloon as it soared into the sky.

About the Author

Bernard Amador is the author of the memoir *To Know Á Fallen Angel: Understanding the Mind of a Sexual Predator* and the novels *The Rut* and *Cyber-Eugenics: The Neural Code.* He is the author of the original screenplays *Used Books* and *No Romance Without Finance.* He is the Supervising Crime Victim Caseworker for the Albany County Crime Victim and Sexual Violence Center and holds a Doctoral degree in Psychology. Dr. Amador organizes The Capital District Screenwriters group and lives in New York City and upstate New York. Visit him at http://www.toknowafallenangel.com

The Fallen Angel, Marc Chagall (1923-1947)

More from Bernard Amador

To Know Å Fallen Angel

POWERFUL BOOK TELLS OF YOUNG BOY'S STRUGGLE NOT TO BECOME A SEXUAL PREDATOR

Being a victim of sexual abuse does not make one a sexual predator but this book presents a case in which it almost does. This is a boldly told coming of age story about how a boy tries not to become a sexual predator. Dr. Amador's treatment is serious yet inspirational. The main theme of his book *To Know A Fallen Angel* is the ability to triumph over the lasting effects of sexual abuse. The book explains what happened to the mind of a sexually abused child and takes its readers on an expedition through the mind of a sexual predator, as the story of a young boy's life unfolds from chapter to chapter. This book gives readers honest insight into the reality of sexual abuse, and the mind of a sexual predator.

Available at **Amazon.com**

Format	Pages	ISBN	Price
Paperback (5.25x8)	216	978-1442152847	11.50

Visit the author at
http://www.toknowafallenangel.com or contact him at bamador@toknowafallenangel.com

More from Bernard Amador

Cyber-Eugenics: The Neural Code

THRILLING NEW SUSPENSE NOVEL DECIPHERS THE NEURAL CODE

The media is full of reports on the recent advances in cognitive science, as researchers ponder the neural code and wonder how it can be deciphered. Eliza Boria is an MIT student who learns that the neural code was already deciphered by the U.S. Government and that the technology to create computer-controlled humans ("Cybernatons") was already tested in the Soviet Union during the Cold War with the first orbit of Sputnik in 1957.
Eliza's grandmother, Bernice Figueroa, traveled to Russia with cybernetic pioneer Norbert Weiner when he gave his lectures on cybernetics and planted the idea of using cybernetics for the advancement of eugenics to create a master race. Eliza finds herself catapulted into the combined efforts of the CIA and FBI to prevent the workings of the neural code from being used by leaders of the underground modern day eugenics movement. When Eliza partakes in a government funded study at MIT that results in the sweltered brains of its subjects, it serves as a warning that deciphering the neural code is a threshold modern day scientists should not cross. Eliza's background has prepared her to be the one to stop the leaders of the modern day eugenics movement from making their diabolical plans a reality.

Available at **Amazon.com**

Format	Pages	ISBN	Price
Paperback (6x9)	252	978-1434854070	15.00

Visit the author at
http://www.toknowafallenangel.com or contact him at bamador@toknowafallenangel.com

More from Bernard Amador

The Rut

A MOOSE ON THE LOOSE AND GAY ADOPTION IN THE NORTH COUNTRY OF NEW YORK

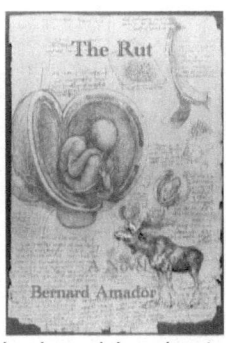

This novel set in the North Country of New York State explores gay adoption in an entertaining way for both gay and general audiences. Gay adoption is becoming more common everyday and is not fully represented in gay fiction. Ean is a young gay man who works as a Forensic Case Manager at a social services agency, who has been married to Stacy, an Assistant District Attorney, for three years. Stacy feels compelled to adopt a child Ean names Tur (Rut spelled backwards), who is about to be placed in foster care. As their journey with Tur begins, Ean almost loses Stacy in a car accident with a male bull moose. Stacy dies suddenly after years of disability. Ean tries to start a new life with Tur without Stacy; however, he encounters many impediments ranging from suicidal thoughts to the Cinderella complex. Ean must overcome the final conflict of allowing Mark, a moose-obsessed Department of Conservation (DEC) worker, to fully enter his life or perish in loneliness. In the end, Ean triumphs as he allows Mark, a new male "bull", into his life.

Available at **Amazon.com**

Format	Pages	ISBN	Price
Paperback (5.25x8)	242	978-0984304028	12.95

Visit the author at
http://www.toknowafallenangel.com or contact him at bamador@toknowafallenangel.com